HARVEST SONG

HARVEST SONG

Ron Hirschi   •   Illustrated by Deborah Haeffele

COBBLEHILL BOOKS/DUTTON · NEW YORK

AUTHOR'S NOTE

THE TIMES I spent with my grandmother are wonderful memories. She also gave me many other memories through stories she told about her childhood. Those stories bring to life the times of our immigrant family. I can almost see Grandma now, as a young child, running to her grandmother's farm just as school lets out in the early spring for planting time...

When school lets out, I run
to Grandma's farm.

When I spend the night, she lets me stay in bed while she rises with the early morning light. She dresses, slips on her tattered slippers, then starts a fire.

The kindling crackles. The dancing fire begins to warm the tiny house. I watch Grandma make breakfast, and when the smell of potato cakes fills every corner of the room, I jump from bed.

Mom cat and her kitten wind around my legs, begging breakfast. I pour milk in their bowl, while Grandma tucks our lunchbasket alongside the garden tools.

After I gather eggs and let the
ducks out of their nighttime
pen, I follow Grandma to the
field along the riverbank.

We walk past bluebirds searching
for a nest and a neighbor's cows
on their hillsides of green. The
cowbells tink, clink. Grandma
hums and I sing the old country
song she has taught me.

One potato for the morning
two for the noonday sun.
One potato for suppertime,
then our day is done.

The first days of gardening are hard work. But Grandma says every season has its chore, every year its own reward. Besides, when the field is dug and hoed, and the soil raked smooth as wheat flour, we go down to the river and fish for our supper.

By the time the bluebirds have found a place to nest, it is time to plant. I help pick out seed potatoes from last year's harvest. Their thick skins are rough and brown like Grandma's hard-working hands.

Grandma slices the seed potatoes, digs small round holes, and I set the pieces in the ground. New plants will grow from the potato eyes that seem to stare up at me as I cover each piece with loose soil.

In a few weeks time, the potato plants begin to grow, sprouting toward the sky. As Grandma plants flowers at the end of each row, I wiggle my toes in the soft, warm soil. I try to touch the new potatoes growing beneath their blanket of earth.

When the sun climbs high above the field, we sit under the elm by the pasture gate and eat our lunch. There is smooth yellow cheese, fresh baked bread, and crunchy apple slices.

All summer long, Grandma weeds the field or
picks asters and zinnias for the neighbors. I water
the flower patch, then run through the potato field,
brushing my hands across the flowers that bloom like
tiny stars in the sky of green.

Too quickly, the blossoms fall....

Grandma says that is how the stars were made—
from all the flowers from seasons past being swept
up into the sky.

By the time it is almost school again, frost sparkles on the morning fields. The neighbors' barns are filled with hay and the baby bluebirds have flown far from their nest. When the potato vines wither and droop, Grandma tells me crumpling vines signal the time for harvest.

As I run through the falling leaves, neighbors help Grandma dig up our potato harvest from beneath the rich soil. The earth smells clean and fresh. In Grandma's hands, the fat potatoes glisten like pieces of gold in the afternoon sun.

We fill many baskets. Some are for winter. Some are for friends. Some are for the next planting season to come. With our cart bulging, we push the potato harvest home.

I help with supper, then sit by Grandma when the neighbors visit with their fiddle, concertina, and apple cider.

When it is time for bed, the cats curl up on my bed. Grandma tucks me in, smoothing the quilt beneath my chin.

As stars twinkle like potato blossoms in the dark
night sky, we sing our harvest song:

One potato for the springtime,
two for the summer sun.
Golden potatoes for wintertime,
now our work is done.

For Nichol...and our loving memories of Nana.   R.H.

For my mother and father, with love.   D.H.

Text copyright © 1991 by Ron Hirschi
Illustrations copyright © 1991 by Deborah Haeffele
All rights reserved. No part of this book may be reproduced
in any form without permission in writing from the publisher.
Library of Congress Cataloging-in-Publication Data
Hirschi, Ron.
Harvest song / Ron Hirschi; illustrated by Deborah Haeffele.
p.   cm.
Summary: A little girl and her grandmother share
many activities together.
ISBN 0-525-65067-9
[1. Grandmothers—Fiction.   2. Country life—Fiction.]
I. Haeffele, Deborah, ill.   II. Title.
PZ7.H59796Har   1991
[E]—dc20   90-27009   CIP   AC
Published in the United States by Cobblehill Books,
an affiliate of Dutton Children's Books,
a division of Penguin Books USA Inc.
Typography by Kathleen Westray
Printed in Hong Kong
First Edition   10 9 8 7 6 5 4 3 2 1